MR. UNIVERSE!

Artist : Keung Chi Kit

（編繪：姜智傑）

Contents

Adventure under the sea!! (Part 8)
海底王國歷險記（8）

Previously on SAMBA FAMILY 5

General Cayman has completed his ascension ceremony, and in order to snatch back the throne for Luna, Kang and Samba confronted the General.

Unfortunately, Luna was caught by Cayman, and the only way to save her was to remove the sword in the stone.

However, this could only be done by a chosen warrior, but even Samba was not able to take it out.

At this moment, Luna brought General Cayman to them...

上回提要：凱曼將軍已經完成登基儀式，剛仔和森巴為了助露娜奪回皇位，與將軍大打出手。不幸地，露娜被凱曼捉去，惟一拯救她的方法是拔出石中神劍。然而，只有被選中的勇者才能把劍拔出，可是連森巴也屢試不果。此時，露娜帶着凱曼將軍來到眾人跟前……

那就是石中神劍。 它是你的了！

露娜！！ 凱曼將軍！你對露娜做甚麼來!?

我只是讓她吸了幾口迷幻煙，
現在她只會聽從我的命令。

露娜，過去和剛仔打招呼吧！ 知道。

剛仔你好。　你沒事吧，露娜!?

抓—

哇！

露娜，是我呀，剛仔！　你不記得我嗎!?

露娜……

她被我催眠了，不會記得任何事!!

可惡呀！

啪—

小子，現在我知道你不是被
選中的勇者，我不會再怕你！

呀~~~

住手!!

你這條陰險的長頸魚！
我實在忍無可忍!!

啊!?你在叫我嗎!?

你令到她不省人事!! 吓！

嘿，不好意思，我想是我稍微重手了……

令到公主昏了過去……

看，你對公主做的事!!

我一定要親自收拾你!!

滾開!!

今日我就要你們全都葬身於此!!

噗—

我是不會輕易放棄!!

嘿!

抓—

I'll bury you with that lousy sword!!

Ahhh ~~

我就將你跟那爛劍埋在一起吧!! 呀~~~ 嗖— 啪—

唭—

Darn it ~~~

可惡呀~~~

I won't give in no matter what!!

Come on !!

無論如何我都不會認輸!! 來吧!!

伏—

甚麼!?你把劍拔出來了!?

他才是被選中的人!?

勇……者

森巴拔不出的石中神劍，
竟然由我拔出來了!?

哼！怎樣都好，
強大的神劍在我手上!!

讓我來打敗你!!　　　嘿!!　　好強的氣勢……

裂—

Huh!?

吓!?

哐—

W...why is it so fragile...!? It cracked into pieces just like that...

Ohh... my sword...!

怎…怎會這麼脆弱……!?就這樣裂成碎片……

噢……我的神劍……!

Could it be because it's been stuck on the stone for too long,

so when once you pulled it out, the years of erosion immediately destroyed it!?

難道它插在石頭裏太久，

由於經年累月的侵蝕，一旦把它拔出來，便立刻破掉了!?

Now even the hilt is longer than the blade... How will I defeat Cayman like this!?

現在劍柄比劍刃還要長……怎用它來擊敗凱曼!?

You want to know how!? Let me teach you!!

Wahhh!!

哇!! 你想知道怎辦!?等我來教你吧!!

哐—

咗— 甚麼!? 我的巨鉗被彈開了!?

哇，果然是把強大的神劍！ 哼！就算你有這東西， 我一樣可以徹底擊敗你!!

咔— 嘿!! 噢—

11

嘿嘿，痛嗎？很抱歉我稍稍用力了……

呀~~~!!

Huh!? You again!

Samba!!

Bite ~~~

吓!?又是你！ 森巴!!

咬～～

It's

yummy

好味

Roar ~~

吼～～

Long

necked

fish

Samba, let's work together to defeat him!!

How did he become like me!?

長頸魚

怎麼他變得像我那樣!?

森巴，我們合力擊敗他!!

Ok

好

呵~~~ 咻— 放屁旋風!?

嘿~~~

砰—

唔~

哼！

凱曼!!我們一對一決鬥吧!! 來吧!!

咔—

哐—

My claw !!

我的鉗!!

Darn it~~ How dare you destroy my claw!!

可惡~~竟敢毀壞我的鉗!!

蓬— 我不會再跟你客氣!!

I won't take it easy on you anymore !!

SWISH—

PO

AH~~

為了人魚之國，我，
龍小剛不會敗給你!!　　噗一

呀~~

Darn
!!

可惡!!

For the sake of the Mermaid Kingdom, I, Long Xiao Kang will not lose to you!!

Speed up!!

全速前進!!

Hey !!

Ahh~~

How did you suddenly become so powerful...!?

嘿!!　　呀~~　　你怎麼突然變得這麼強大……!?

噢一　　　　　呵~~~　　　　　　吓!?又是你!?　　　　　呀~~~

轟一

蓬~~　　　　　剛仔！森巴！

嘎~　　　國皇！　你們沒事就好了！

我們終於打敗凱曼將軍，
救回人魚之國⋯⋯　　　　但我不能呼吸⋯⋯　　　剛仔!!

PHEW

呼—

I'm back!

我回來了!

Phelps!!

菲比斯!!

Why are you here!?

怎麼你在這裏!?

Oh... what smelly breath ~~~

噢……好臭的氣息~~~

Ah!

啊!

After you guys entered the palace, I gathered many strong ocean friends of mine to break through the palace gate.

你們進入皇宮之後,我找來很多強壯的海洋朋友,一起攻破皇宮的大門。

What's more, we caught all the bad fish warriors and released all the fish who were being held captive.

還有,我們把所有惡魚士兵捉起來,也釋放了所有被俘虜的人魚。

We have successfully taken back the control of the palace!!

我們成功取回皇宮的控制權了!!

Good job, Phelps!!

做得好,菲比斯!!

YEAH!

好極!

Ah! There's still one more thing that we haven't settled...

呀!還有一件事未解決呀……

We need to wake Luna up!!

我們要救醒露娜!!

魷魚!你最好告知我們怎樣救醒露娜公主!!

Squid! You'd better tell us how to wake Princess Luna up!!

I swear I don't know! Only General Cayman knows how~~

But there's one method we can try...

我發誓我不知道!只有凱曼將軍才知道~~

但有一個方法可以試……

Get the chosen warrior to give the princess a kiss!

就是勇者給公主一個吻!

Ah? Give princess ...

a kiss...!?

啊?給公主……

一個吻……!?

This is it, Kang!

I'd better kiss her quickly!

去吧,剛仔!

快些親下去!

20

Though there's a bubble in between, I'm still so nervous...

雖然隔着個氣泡，但依然好緊張呀……

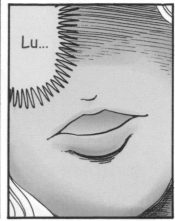

Lu...

露……

PUZZZ

嘆一

Ah? What happened?

呀？發生甚麼事？

Ha～～～

Samba! Look what you have done!!

I'm happy that you woke up, daughter~

Is the Mermaid Kingdom safe now!?

Yes~

哈～～～

森巴！看你做的好事!!

你醒過來就好了，乖女～

人魚之國沒事了!?

是呀～

Samba!!

Ha～～～

森巴!!

哈～～～

Good-bye

Fat

Fish

I must go back to the sea to settle my kingdom's affairs, thank you for saving the Mermaid Kingdom, Kang!

Princess, oh no... I should call you Queen Luna... Will we meet again someday?

再見　　肥魚　　我要回去海底處理國務，感謝你拯救了人魚之國，剛仔！　　公主，不……該是露娜女皇……我們還會再見嗎？

Don't worry, I'll come to visit you some day when I'm free!

I'll wait for you, Luna!

CHU~~

放心，他日有空的話，我就會來找你們！　　我等你了，露娜！　　嗯~~　　我又呼

Ahhh~~ I'm so dizzy now...

Wahhh~~ Kang just fainted!!

Let Phelps perform CPR on him!!

Wahh~ go away~~

Let

me

do

呀~~我暈了……　　哇~~剛仔突然暈了!!　　讓菲比斯幫他做人工呼吸!!　　哇~走開呀~~

You're Mr. Universe! (Part 1)
你是宇宙先生！（1）

嗚……16！　呀……17！　唏……18！　　　　　　　　　　　嘿……19！

嘎～終於完成了 20 次舉重！

砰—　　　　　　　　　　　　　　　　　　　　哇～～～救命啊！！
　　　　　　　　　　　　　　　　　　　　　　壓死我了！

24

SWIFT

Ah...

伏一　　　　呀……

Hey

Thank you, fitness trainer Samba~

嘿　　　　謝謝你，森巴健身教練~

Accep- tance check

Checking it so quickly again!?

量 進 度　　　這麼快又量嗎!?

25cm, 1cm more than yesterday.

25 厘米，比昨天多了 1 厘米。

Train again

Yes sir!

再練　　　　　　是，教練！

Booo, I'm such a poor thing...

嗚，為何我會這麼辛苦……

25

Two days ago

兩日前

5 km/h

Pant pant ...

嘎嘎……

I feel so good jogging in such cool autumn weather!

I've been running for an hour, let's take a break.

Let's keep running

秋高氣爽，這個天氣跑步真舒服！

我已跑了一小時，休息一下吧。

繼續跑

Hey! The cute guys over there!

噢！前面兩位可愛的孩子！

That's right you two! You've been shortlisted as one of members of the universe power group!

就是你們兩個！你們已被選為宇宙戰團的一員了！

In search of a man with the most perfect build and intelligence, the Mr. Universe Competition is here!

The champion will be crowned "Mr. Universe". What's more, the prize money of a million dollars will be his too!

為了找出世上最完美、美貌與智慧並重的男人，再次舉行宇宙先生選舉！

冠軍除了被冠以「宇宙先生」之名，更可獨得 100 萬獎金！

Quick, accept the 14th Mr. Universe challenge!

MR.UNIVERSE

快來接受第十四屆宇宙先生選舉的挑戰吧！

宇宙先生

Don't hesitate, come grab the registration form!

Mr. Universe Competition?

別考慮了，快來索取報名表格吧！

宇宙先生選舉？

Haha, this kind of competition is totally not for me.

I'm not a macho man, I'm only a primary school student ...

哈哈，這種比賽怎會適合我。

我又不是肌肉男，只是小學生而已……

HUD

I am in

伏—

我參加

27

Samba, you're too young to join.

Huh

森巴你年紀太小，不能參加。

吓

But you could nominate your brother Kang to take part!

How did you know my name?

Ya

不過你可以提名你的哥哥剛仔參加！

你怎會知道我的名字？

呀～～

And the person who makes the nomination is entitled to a free ice-cream!

Hey

Wow

Don't ignore me

提名人更可免費得到軟雪糕一個！

喂～～

嘩

別無視我～～

Why do you have my personal details!?

Form
Name : Long Xiao Kang
Age : 12
Occupation : Student

Please sign here.

在這裏簽名吧。

報名表　姓名：龍小剛
年齡：12　職業：學生

你怎會有我的個人資料!?

I was the one who told him.

是我告訴他的。

Wow~~
Dad!

啊~~爸爸！

Samba
baby!

Daddy

Dad,
why
you
dressed
like
that?

森巴兒子！ 爸~~~ 爸爸，你怎會
穿成禧樣？

Your mom is busy
doing research,
so I created the
campaign.

Cam-
paign...
That
cam-
paign!?

你的媽媽忙着做研究，
所以我就辦選舉。

選舉……
這選舉!?

That's right!
He's the
ambassador
for Mr.
Universe.

The first
Mr. Universe~
James!

Hey!!

對！他就是本屆宇宙先生的
宣傳大使。

第一屆宇宙先生
冠軍~占士！

嘿!!

As his son,
you must
take part
in the
championship!

But I don't
want to join!

Kang~

你身為他的兒子，
當然要參加比賽！

但我不想參加！

剛仔~

You're 12 years old already, old enough to take this challenge!

This competition is an opportunity for you! Since you inherited my perfect genes, you must surely win the championship!

Argh~~

你今年已經十二歲，是時候接受這個挑戰！

這次選舉是個好機會！你遺傳了我的優良基因，一定能奪冠！

嗚啊~~

Samba and Monkey, you will be Kang's personal trainers!

Get him into tip-top shape!

Yes

森巴和馬騮，你們做剛仔的教練！

讓他擁有完美體形！　是

I have to tour the world to promote the campaign.

我還要巡迴世界宣傳。

See you in 10 days at the competition!

Work hard Kang!

我們十日後在比賽時再見！

努力吧，剛仔！

What's going on here anyway...

Let the training start

究竟發生甚麼事……

開始訓練

就這樣，我就開始了
地獄式特訓……

嗚~~~~~

呼呼

哈~~~~

哈哈！

唏！ 唏！

呼~~~~

登登

Hey, I've grown bigger after training, haven't I?

嘿，我經過鍛煉後，就長肌肉了，對吧？

THUD

砰一

How did he get bigger than me without training!?

Ho

Maybe he's got better genes from James than you.

為何他沒鍛煉也長了一身肌肉!?

呵

可能他比你遺傳了更多占士的優良基因。

But your physique is still not perfect. Let me help you out.

不過你的身型仍未完美，讓我來幫你吧。

Macho man milk powder!!

肌肉男奶粉 !!　　　　　　　　肌肉男

This muscle building milk powder was developed by your mom.

這是你媽媽研發的肌肉增強奶粉。

You can become even more muscular after drinking it! Up to 180% bigger!

喝了後就能令你肌肉發達！增幅多達 180%！

Samba, please feed this to Kang!

Come

come

I don't want to be a lab rat!

森巴，餵剛仔喝吧！　　來吧　　我不想當白老鼠！

Drink

Arrr

喝　　　　嗚～～～

喝完　　　嗯～～　　　嘿！這樣餵他，要當心⋯⋯

嗯～～　　　有甚麼感覺!?

沒有。　　　看來沒有變化。

啊—！

嗚啊～～　　　我的臉發生甚麼事？

嘆──!!

Why did it only affect my face!?

Ha~

Haha, this proves that it's a failed experiment.

為甚麼只有臉有效果!?

哈~~

哈哈,證明實驗失敗了。

Eh?

Your arm hair is growing fast.

咦?

你的手長了很多毛髮。

Hairy macho man? That's so out-dated.

I suggest you better shave it off.

No, I don't want to!

多毛肌肉男?真老土。

我建議你脫毛比較好。

不,我不想做!

完成

大家各就各位！

預備......

撕 !!!

哇~~~~

嘎......嘎......

很痛一！　　　　　　我要報仇!!　　哇～～～現在你皮光肉滑，　　　　真的嗎!?　　　　　對，連臉也回復正常了。
　　　　　　　　　　　　　　　　　很英俊呀……

啊～～～　　　　　　　　　　真的變得英俊了～

為何我的頭髮會變成這樣!?　　　換個髮型不是很好嗎……　　別擔心，我們找了五星級髮型師　　　你好。
　　　　　　　　　　　　　　　　　　　　　　　　　　　　企鵝先生為你弄好些。

這個髮型夠新潮嗎？　　哇~~　　唔……

這個。　　甚麼來的!?

這個又怎樣……　　啊？　　好　　就是它！

接着就做護膚面膜！

以及修指甲和腳甲。

然後森巴替你畫點肌肉。

我呢？就為你做戰衣！

改造完成！

每個人都在注視我這新造型！

入口
Entry

那是誰？　　他的衣服真老土。　　　　　　　　　他是來參選的嗎？

宇宙先生選舉即將開始!!

待續。

You're Mr. Universe! (Part 2)
你是宇宙先生！（2）

Previously, Kang was forced to participate in the "Mr. Universe" competition. After a series of hellish training, the competition will finally be starting tonight! Will he win or not!?

上回提到，剛仔被逼參加「宇宙先生選舉」，經過一輪地獄式訓練，比賽終於在今晚開始，他會否贏得比賽呢!?

Today, they are going to fight for the title of Mr. Universe!

今天，他們會競逐宇宙先生的殊榮！

Ladies and gentlemen, welcome to the 14th Mr. Universe competition.

This time, we've had thousands of hunks taking part in the competition, but only 8 of them qualified for the finals!!

Today, they are going to fight for the title of Mr. Universe!

今次比賽有過千名猛男參加，但晉身決賽的只有八位!!

I am the master of ceremonies De Niro!!

There will be 3 rounds of challenges in the game.

In each round, we will eliminate some contestants until the champion is chosen!!

各位觀眾，歡迎來到第十四屆宇宙先生選舉的現場。

我是大會司儀迪尼路!!

比賽共分為三個回合。

每個回合都會淘汰部分選手，直至冠軍誕生!!

現場 500 位女觀眾會成為評判。　嘩～～　迪尼路你很帥啊 !!　　你們的掌聲和歡呼聲都是令他們晉級的關鍵 !!

你們的聲音會由三位聲音分析專家去辨識。　再得出一個分數，去決定選手的名次 !!　所以看到心儀的猛男，就大叫去支持他吧 !!

嘩～～　哈～～　　耶～～　我愛你　很帥啊～～　哈～～

好，事不宜遲，讓我介紹八位宇宙先生選手出場吧 !!

伏伏伏伏——— 　　　砰～～～ 　　　　　呵～～～

你是誰？為何走上台!? 　　我要玩

我是屁屁獸 超級宇宙戰士

選手親屬請返回座位。 　　保安！幫我抓住他!! 　　　　　　決鬥吧

碰—　　　　　　喝　啪—　　　　　　　很痛！　　　　　　嗚～

森巴，看我買了甚麼給你吃。

來，跟我到觀眾席　　　好呀
享受美食吧!!

嚼嚼　　　　　　哈～～～

好，有請八位選手出場～~!!

Contestant number 5, gold medal otaku, Ming!!

Age: 18
Height: 123cm
Weight: 42kg
Occupation: Student
Hobby: Internet, video games, comic books

年齡：18 身高：123 厘米 體重：42 公斤 職業：學生 嗜好：上網、電玩、看動漫

Contestant number 6, the uncle who never gets old, Simon!!

六號選手，寶刀未老阿伯西蒙 !! 年齡：103 身高：155 厘米 體重：32 公斤 職業：退休人士 嗜好：算術

Age: 103
Height: 155cm
Weight: 32kg
Occupation: Retiree
Hobby: Maths

Contestant number 7, king of the beasts, Lion!!

Contestant number 8, descendent of former champion, Long Xiao Kang!!

Eh? Why does that uncle look so much like Uncle Johnny!?

咦？為甚麼那個阿伯這麼像阿伯莊尼 !?

Age: 24
Height: 178cm
Weight: 120kg
Occupation: Zoo manager
Hobby: Hunting

Age: 12
Height: 153cm
Weight: 39kg
Occupation: Student
Hobby: Being bullied by younger brother

七號選手，
萬獸之王賴恩 !! 年齡：24 身高：178 厘米 體重：120 公斤 職業：動物園經理 嗜好：獵食

八號選手，
冠軍後裔龍小剛 !! 年齡：12 身高：153 厘米 體重：39 公斤 職業：學生 嗜好：被弟弟欺負

八位猛男已準備接受挑戰了!!　　　　事不宜遲，立刻開始比賽吧!!

第一回合!!　　　　泳裝環節!!

為了表現宇宙先生應有的健美身型，　　各位戰士會穿上泳裝讓觀眾評分！　　嘩~~~　　太好了!!

各位選手，你們有兩分鐘時間
準備，現在開始，關燈！

啪一

請換上大會提供的泳褲 !!　　　　　唔……　　　　　　　　　這太小了吧 !!

哈 ~~~ 很合身呀 ~~

幸好我有準備……

看，我自己的泳褲很好吧？　　　　　還有一分鐘 !!

嘩 !! 為何這麼光？已經開燈了嗎 !?

49

Wah!! Your body is shining!?

Hey, want to try it out?

嘩 !! 你全身在發光 !?

咦，你也想試嗎？

You can't say I'm not generous!

Wah!!

別説我吝嗇了！

哇 !!

After applying this oil, your skin will be smooth and your muscles will appear firmer!

Really!?

塗上油後，你的皮膚會很光滑，肌肉看上去也更結實！

真的嗎 !?

Wow, it really works! My body looks different now!

嘩，真有效！我的身體有很大改變！

Humph, I can have same effect without that oil, see!!

The fair and shining skin~~

Human light tube!?

哼，我不用塗油也有相同效果啊 !!

皮膚白得反光 ~~

人肉光管 !?

啪—　　有請一號、二號選手上場!!　　擺出最有自信的姿勢吧!!　　嘩～～

啼～～～　　　　　　　　　　　　　　　　　哈～～

現場觀眾反應熱烈，分數愈來愈高了!!　　究竟兩位選手得到多少分呢?　　首先評分給一號選手，鐵木金!!　　請大叫!!

Silence reigns~~~

鴉雀無聲～～

鐵木金得到兩分！！

Woody got 2 points !!

Seems like the ladies don't like the oily look on him!!

Booo~~~

嗚～～

女士似乎不太喜歡他滿身油的造型！！

Were the cheers just now for another person!?

Contestant number 2, pretty boy, Thors!! Screaming please!!

難道之前的呼聲是給另一人的!?

二號選手，美少年托爾斯！！請大叫！！

果然沒錯！！公佈成績吧！！

Wow ？～？

Thors !!

I love you ♥

嘩～～～

托爾斯！！

我愛你

Sure enough, right!! Let's check out the rating!!

Yeah~~

Whee~~~

Wow!!

26 points! Will he qualify for the next round!?

耶～

嘩～～～

嘩！！

26分！看來他會順利出線吧!?

賴恩先生，現時在比賽，能否請你放下獸性一會？

Mr. Lion, we're in a competition now, could you please hide your beast?

Wah ~~~~ Help!!

哇 ~~~~ 救命呀 !!

THROW!

嘆一

Contestant number 7, Lion!!

Screaming please!!

Roar!!

七號選手，賴恩 !!

請大叫 !!

吼 !!

Errrr...

唔......

Looks like Lion has terrified the audiences...

......

看來賴恩已嚇壞了觀眾……

Roar~~!! Those who don't scream, will be eaten by me!!

Wah!!

Argh

吼~~!! 誰不叫我就吃了她!!

哇!! 呀~~

Yeah, this is it.

Wow!!

Lion!!

對，就是這樣。

嘩!! 賴恩!!

Wow! Lion got 26 points!!

He will qualify for sure!!

嘩！賴恩得到 26 分!!

肯定能出線了!!

Now, the last remaining contestant,

Number 8 Long Xiao Kang! Oh, are you dropping out of the contest?

現在剩下最後一位選手，

八號龍小剛！看來你要退出比賽了？

No, I'm not.

I'm going to continue, OK!!

不退啊。

我要繼續，好嗎!!

I'm number 8, Long Xiao Kang!!

Everybody... Show time!!

我是八號，龍小剛!!

各位觀眾……看我表演!!

Hey!!

唏 !!

Ha!!

嘿 !!

Woosh !!

呵 !!

Wow!! Fantastic performance!! I believe you'll score really well!

Screaming please!!

Thank goodness the days of harsh training were not in vain...

嘩!!表演很精彩!!
我相信你一定能取
得好成績！

請大叫!!

那數天的艱辛訓練
總算沒有白費……

The pose is so weird...

His hair style is so gross...

No muscle at all, and he's so short...

Thors is much better than you...

姿勢很奇怪……　　髮型很醜……　　沒有肌肉，而且很矮……　　托爾斯比你好得多……

Oh, I can sense a lukewarm reaction from the audiences...

Only got a few claps out of sympathy...

Clap

...

...

...

Clap

...

噢，看來觀眾的反應很冷淡……　　啪　　啪　　只有幾下同情的掌聲……

Booo... I've been working so hard on this, but there's no cheering for me at all...

...

Seems like this time I've really failed...

嗚……我這麼努力，但一點歡呼聲也沒有……　　看來這次輸定了……

Kang

Wow

You're so stylish!!

Clap Clap Clap

剛　你很有型!!　嘩　啪啪啪

Samba!! Monkey!!

You go, Kang!!

Go

go

森巴!! 馬騮!!　　加油，剛仔!!　　好　好

57

Wow!!

哔 !!

Wow!! The judges were all touched by his family love!!

Number 8 Long Xiao Kang got 26 points and he's just somehow qualifies for the final four!!

哔!!評判都被他們的親情感動 !!

八號龍小剛得到26分,順利進入四強 !!

Along with number 2, 3, and 7, these 4 contestants are heading for all-out war!!

Yay!!

After a word from our sponsors, round 2 will begin!!

連同二號、三號和七號,
四位選手將會展開一輪激戰 !!

耶 !!

廣告後開始第二回合 !!

Advertisement

Men's hair removal cream

Seal Brand

You'll be as smooth as an egg!!

廣告　海狗牌　男士脱毛膏　令你如雞蛋般光滑 !!

Booo... I will not admit defeat so easily...

嗚……我不會就此
認輸的……

You're Mr. Universe! (Part 3)
你是宇宙先生！（3）

Ladies and gentlemen, welcome back to the Mr. Universe Competition !!

I believe you all are very impatient now !!

各位觀眾，歡迎再次來到宇宙先生的比賽現場 !!

相信大家已心急如焚 !!

Yeah~~~!!

耶~~~!! 剛

After witnessing the warriors' looks and figures, now I am going to test their intelligence!!

Round two~ "The Quiz" begins!! Let's welcome the final four!!

看完所有戰士的美貌與身材後，現在要考驗他們的智慧了 !!

第二回合「問答環節」開始 !! 有請四強 !!

Wah~~ Oh~~~~~ Ah~~ Handsome boy~~~

BANG Wah~~~ Come on!!

嘩~~~ 砰—— 噢~~~~~~ 呀~~ 嘩~~~ 帥哥~~~ 來吧 !!

走開，不准騷擾參賽者！　　哇~~　　啪——

保安！制止這羣瘋狂的擁躉‼　　是！　　哇~~我的頭髮！　　退後！退後！　　嘎~~

好！危機解除！第二回合正式開始‼　　呼~~

我會隨機抽選一條問題問每位戰士。　　好，三號沙格，聽清楚了！　　好‼

甚麼⁉

三隻小雞和兩隻貓……

陳先生想用木筏把一隻獅子、兩隻貓、三隻小雞運到對岸。除了自己，木筏只能坐兩隻動物。但是沒人的時候，如果貓和獅子數量相同，獅子就會吃了貓；小雞和貓數量相同或少於貓時，貓就會吃了小雞。請問要把所有動物順利送到對岸，最少要渡河多少次？

一、二、三、四……

答案是 16!!　　錯!!是 7 次!!　　答案差太遠了！沒智慧是不配做宇宙先生的!!　　淘汰!!　哇～～　砰一　下一位!!

好！一加一等於……？　　　　　　　　二!!

沒錯！答案是二！　耶!!　托爾斯最強　二號托爾斯果然不負眾望，順利出線！　　謝謝!!　問題是隨機抽選的，很公平啊！

Alright! Contestant 7, Lion, your question is ~~~~

Please calculate the following formula and tell us the answer!

$$\frac{\sqrt{y^2 + 2x^2 + 39} - \sqrt{3x}}{\frac{1}{3} + \left(\frac{2}{7}\right)^x} = \frac{x^2 - y^2}{8}$$

$x = ?$ $y = ?$

好！七號賴恩，你的問題是 ~~~~ 　　請計算出以下算式的答案！

Roar~~~~

How could I answer such a difficult question? I've never learnt maths before!!

Wah! Security!!

POP

吼 ~~~~ 　我怎懂得回答這麼難的問題？
我沒有學過數學!!　　　哇！保安!!　　　卜一

Back Stage

Alright! The last warrior!

Contestant 8, Kang! Listen carefully!!

後台　　　　　　好！最後一位戰士！　　　八號剛仔！聽清楚!!

63

Three things suddenly fall from the sky and hit your head, which one would cause more harm to you?

1) A 2 pounds durian

2) A 3 kg hammer

3) A 8 x 12 inch wooden table

1) 一個兩磅重的榴槤　2) 一個三公斤的鐵鎚　3) 一張八乘十二吋的木枱

Oh no~~~ I wouldn't know how to solve this riddle...

I'm so poor in maths...

糟了 ~~~ 我不懂得這題目……　　我的數學這麼差……

3 kg is 6 pounds ~~~~

Uhhh... The answer is...

三公斤等於六磅 ~~~~　　呃……答案是……

That's right! The answer is your head !!

對！答案就是你的頭 !!

Seems like this IQ question wasn't difficult for you!

Kang, you've qualified for the next round!!

Oh yeah? I seriously have no idea what happened or how I made it... But I passed!

看來這條 IQ 題也難不到你！　　剛仔你晉級了 !!　　真好？完全不知道發生甚麼事……但過關了！

Everybody, the final two contestants of Mr. Universe are here!

The finals is about to start!

各位，宇宙先生最後兩強選手已經誕生！

決賽即將開始！

暫停 PAUSE

?

Oh?

呀？

只要他們擲到的數字大於一，就能重回比賽!!

In order to give another chance to the rest,

a special "redemption" round begins now!!

What?

If anyone of them rolls a number more than 1, then they are back into the game!!

What a weird rule!!

為了給其他選手多一次機會，

特別「復活」環節開始!!

甚麼？

規則真馬虎!!

噗— 啪— 啪—

你有問題嗎？那豈不是重頭來過？

Wow!! All the warriors are back in the game!!

Swimsuit round 2.0 starts!!

Hey what's wrong with you? The competition has restarted again?

Hahaha ... please give others some chance...

嘩!! 全部戰士復活!!

泳裝環節 2.0 開始!!

哈哈哈……多給其他人機會呀……

This time, all the warriors will perform their most outstanding moves to us!!

Let's welcome contestant 1, Iron Woody for his fitness performance !!

這次各位戰士會表演他的拿手項目 !!

有請一號選手鐵木金表演健身 !!

嗚~~~ 插！

呀~~~很痛~~~!!　　　　　　　為何地上會有釘子!?

啊!!一號選手發生意外，被自己的啞鈴打中了!!

噹一

噗!!　　　　　　啊~~~

雖然發生了意外，但比賽仍會繼續！有請二號選手托爾斯！

他昏倒了！　　　　　　看來他要退出比賽！

嘩~~~　　嘩~~~~~~

He will perform his best act~ Ballet!

Let's get wet!

Ladies, scream ~~~~!

他會表演最擅長的芭蕾舞！　來弄濕吧！　各位女士，尖叫吧~~~~!

Hmm? Why is the water so hot?

唔？這水怎會這麼熱？

Wahhh~~ Is this chili oil!? So hot ~~~~

Wahhh~~ What's wrong with Thors!?

So embar-rassing...

哇~~~ 這是辣椒油嗎？很熱呀~~~~　很醜……　哇~~托爾斯發生甚麼事!?

啊！二號選手托爾斯退出比賽了！

Wah I quit !!

Oh! Contestant 2, Thors just quit the game!

Ah~~

Out

呀，我退出啊！　退出　啊~~

Contestant 3, Sager is going to perform wood chopping !

Out

三號選手沙格會表演劈木板！　退出

Contestant 4, Master Shen is bringing us his harmonica solo!

Out

退出　四號選手沈大師表演口琴獨奏！

Unfortunately, the warriors kept having horrible performance. But, let's see what amazing action that contestant 5, Ming will show us?

He's going to show us his computer graphics !!

很不幸地，選手相繼失準，五號選手阿明會帶給我們甚麼精彩演出呢？

他會表演電腦繪畫 !!

CLICK

CLICK

CLICK

CLICK

CLICK

噠噠噠噠噠

TA DAH———

登登———

$\frac{1}{2}$ 0.5   0

Although there's no reaction from the audiences, he has the highest points so far!

Will he be crowned Mr. Universe this year !?

Thank you!

雖然觀眾反應冷淡，但他暫時得分最高！

他會勝出今屆的宇宙先生嗎!?

謝謝！

Hehe, I'm sure win this time!

嘿嘿，我贏定了！

69

嗚～～爸爸～～我無論如何也要贏得冠軍！　　好，乖兒子不要哭，我一定會幫你贏的！　　只要用點錢就能解決了！　　這是給你的，請關照一下我的兒子！　　好，沒問題！

只要其他對手都退出了，

只剩下我一個，就肯定能得到冠軍了！　　那你為何讓所有人復活？　　這樣做就不會有人發現是我指使的！　　豈有此理!!　　原來你就是黑幕!!　哇!!

有請六號選手西蒙！　　　　大家好 ~~~

呀……我想看他的表演……　　　可惡 ~~~~

他會為我們表演踩汽水罐 !!　　　我要踩十個 !!

卡一

砰 !!

哇 !! 汽水罐爆炸了 !!　　　又一位戰士犧牲了！

Alright! Next warrior, Lion!!

好！下一位戰士，賴恩！！

He's been knocked out by a powerful sleeping drug.

他中了強力安眠藥而昏迷。

Now, there's only one warrior left, number 8!

現在剩下最後的戰士了，八號！

Darn, using such dirty tricks to tarnish the competition...

I cannot fall into his trap and let his rich son win the championship!

可惡，以這些卑鄙手段來玷污比賽……

如果我也失手，就會讓那二世祖拿到冠軍！

In the name of my father, James, I will defeat you!!

以我父親占士的名義，我要打敗你！！

Wahhh~~ What a strong force! Just like his father!

What is he going to perform!?

哇～～很強的氣勢！就像他的父親啊！

他想表演甚麼!?

火‼

咘咘咘

呵～～～

一起來跳火火舞！　　哈哈～～～　哈哈～～～　　嘩！龍小剛的自創舞蹈
　　　　　　　　　　　　　　　　　　　很受歡迎啊‼

快！阻止他跳！　　是‼

SWISH

伏——

Wah! I can't see any-thing !!

哇！甚麼都看不見 !!

BANG

Go away !!

砰——　　滾開 !!

Wow!! What an exciting fighting performance !!

Ladies and gentlemen, applause please !!

嘩 !! 非常精彩的格鬥技表演 !!　各位觀眾，請鼓掌 !!

Haha, looks like I'll be the champion!

哈哈，看來冠軍是我的了 !

You wish, don't forget the judges were bribed by me!

What!?

你想得美，別忘記我收買了評判呀 !　　甚麼 !?

啊！

I have complaint! They are fake judges!!

Really? I can't tell...

Hi

我要投訴！他們是假評判!!

真的嗎？我看不出來......

嗨

舅舅，幫我拿回冠軍!!

Uncle, help me get back my championship!!

Don't worry, I'll take care of it!

放心，我會幫你的！

Get out from here both of you!!

BANG

你們兩個快給我滾!!

砰一

I finally beat others with my own strength!!

Wow! What a spectacular performance! The Mr. Universe champion has finally been unveiled!

The winner goes to...

我終於憑自己的實力打敗對手!!

嘩！很精彩的表演！宇宙先生冠軍終於揭盅了！

冠軍就是......

Samba～～～!

Ha—

What!? Why?

森巴～～～!　　　哈—　　　甚麼!? 為甚麼?

Samba's lifelike appearance made me think he was the real judge,

what an amazing act by Samba! He deserves the championship!!

Ha

森巴的扮相維妙維肖，連我也以為他是真評判，　　哈　　森巴的表演這麼精彩！他拿冠軍是實至名歸!!

後台　　這故事真荒唐啊……

Back stage

This is truly the most ridiculous story ever...

Waiting to give the award

等待頒獎

A doodle battle
塗鴉大戰

大家好~~~~

完成

是甚麼？　　　　　我知！是一隻麻雀!!

錯 是垃圾　　　　吓~~~？

可惡！到我畫了!!

啪——

完成！猜猜這是甚麼!?

我 知 是 石頭

錯!!　　　　　是我的耳屎!!　　　　呀~~~~

啪——　好!! 我們決鬥吧!!　啪——

森巴對兜巴哥!!　　　　　　第三百二十三回，開始!!

畫完

這是甚麼　　　　　　我知!! 又是垃圾!!

錯 是 麻雀　　　　　吓～～～?

80

哼!!到我畫了!!

啪——

畫完!! 這是甚麼!?

我知 是 兜巴哥

錯!!　　　　　　這也是我的耳屎!!　　呀~~~

啪——　　好!!我們再鬥過!!　　啪——

你們兩個停手啊!! 啪—— 砰—— 玩夠了吧!!

看你們浪費了多少紙張!?

還有你!看這兩頁根本一模一樣呀! 你想騙稿費嗎!?

你們知道需要砍伐大量樹木, 才造得到紙!?

All the forests on earth are disappearing one by one, if they are gone, these won't be any trees to produce oxygen and absorb carbon dioxide, and our air will get more polluted!

Soon, the earth will no longer be suitable for us to live in!! And all mankind will perish!!

地球上的森林一個接一個消失，失去樹木製造氧氣和吸收二氧化碳，空氣污染就會愈來愈嚴重！

那時候，地球就再不適合我們居住!!所有人類將會滅亡!!

Oh

So what?

Then why aren't you stopping!?

哦　　那又如何？　　你們還要繼續!?

Can you please find another way to battle? Don't waste any more paper!!

PA !!

你們用另一種方式決鬥好嗎？別再浪費紙了!!　啪!!

......

Alright! Then let's see who can take off Kang's clothes faster!!

Hey!! Leave me out of this!!

Ha

好！那我們鬥快脫掉剛仔的衣服吧!!　喂!!別拿我來鬥!!　哈

83

It's a tie

Let's do it again

again

Fine!! Then let's see who can tickle Kang the most!!

Hey Stop!!

I think you should just resume your doodle battle.

And this time I can be the judge, OK?

Hmmm, OK

又 平手 再鬥過　好!! 這次看誰最能使剛仔覺得癢!!　停止啊!!　你們還是鬥畫畫吧。　這次我來當評判，好嗎？　嗯，好吧~~~

Alright, my goal for you is...

to draw the greatest super hero or monster you can think of !!

好，我的題目是……　畫出你們心目中最強的超級英雄或怪獸!!

Dubar Gor you draw the super hero, and Samba you draw the monster!!

The best drawing will be today's winner!!

OK!! Samba VS Dubar Gor,

Round 325 begins!!

兜巴哥畫超級英雄，森巴就畫怪獸!!　畫得最好的就是今天的優勝者!!　好!!森巴對兜巴哥，　第三百二十五回開始!!

遊戲攻略

Hey

唏~~~~~

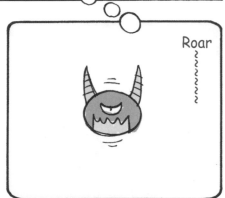

Roar

吼~~~~~

Hey

唏~~~~~

Roar

吼~~~~~

Hey

唏~~~~~

Roar

吼~~~~~~

Hey
~~~~~

Roar
~~~~~

啤~~~~

吼~~~~

Hey
~~~~~~~

Roar
~~~~~~

啤~~~~

吼~~~~~

Hey
~~~~~~~

Roar
~~~~~

啤~~~~

吼~~~~~

Hey
~~~~~~

Roar
~~~~~

啤~~~~~

吼~~~~~

Hey

啼~~~~~

Roar

吼~~~~

Hey

啼~~~~~

Roar

吼~~~~

Hey

啼~~~~~

Roar

吼~~~~~

Hey

啼~~~~~

Roar

吼~~~~~~

畫完!!　　　呵

唏～～～　　　吼 吼　　　你們兩人的程度果然相近……

啪——　　　這個回合平手!!　　　啪——

既然無法分勝負，來下一個回合吧!! 好 　　題目是~~~~

請畫出我龍小剛的帥臉。 　　誰畫得更帥就能勝出!!

完成~~~

再見　　　　　再見~~~　　　　喂，不要走啊!!

你們畫我畫得太隨便了吧!!　　　　　　　　　我是這本漫畫的主角呀，好嗎!?!

You should draw me like a dashing hero,

你們應該把我畫成英俊瀟灑的英雄,

or portray me as a muscular man!

或描繪成肌肉男!

You can even draw me in a cute animated version!!

甚至畫成可愛的漫畫風都可以!!

No matter what you draw,

the most important thing is that you draw with your passion!!

無論你們想怎樣畫,

最重要是用熱情來作畫!!

哇~~~!!

剛　　　龍小剛

嘿——

嘿——

哈~~~

哈哈~~~　　　你們為何在傻笑？

完 成

Samba is wearing glasses!?
森巴戴眼鏡!?

The Moon
ZZZ

月亮

TATATAT~~~
CLANK~~~

噠噠噠~~~

哐~~~

Wow~~ this 3D game is really something !!
The character really seems like it is popping out from the screen !!

哇~~這台3D遊戲機真厲害!!

角色逼真得就像會
從畫面裏跳出來!!

過關

STAGE CLEAR
LV UP
TA-DAH~~~
Level 9!
HP+12! / ATK+7! / DEF+10!

Yeah!! I've gained another level!!
3D games are so fun!!

登登~~~ LV UP= Level Up 升級 等級9！ HP=Hit Point/ Health Point 生命值 ATK=Attack 攻擊 DEF=Defence 防禦

太好了!!又過了一關!!

3D遊戲真好玩!!

Phew~~~ but my eyes are sore now after playing it for a long stretch...

I should take a break now...

Hm?

嘎~~~ 不過玩久了，眼睛開始發痛……　　　還是休息一下吧……　　　　　　　　唔？

Ha~~~

Don't sit so close to the TV!! It will damage your eyesight!!

Wah~~~

I want to watch

哈~~~　　　　　　　　　　　　　　　　不要坐得太近電視機!! 哇~~~ 我 要 看
　　　　　　　　　　　　　　　　　　它會損害你的視力!!

?

剛早晨

你看我時怎麼瞇着眼？

森巴可能有近視！

吓！不是吧？

森巴，跟我來！

我要給你做個視力測試！

這個箭頭指向哪？

這個又指向哪？

那這個呢？

你連這麼大的箭頭也看不到？
我想你患了嚴重近視……

哈~~~

最近，我看你不單貼近螢幕來看
電視，看書時也不開燈！唉，小
小年紀便有近視真差勁……

Let's go get you a pair of glasses!

我現在帶你去配一副
眼鏡吧！

THUD

砰—

What are you doing? That's so scary!!

This is an ancient eye therapy from the Guru tribe,

just soak two peacocks' feathers in frog's tears for 10 minutes, then cover them over your eyes after they dry out. I'm sure this will help your near-sightedness!

你們在幹甚麼？
這很嚇人!!

這個是咕嚕族的
原始療眼法，

只要把兩條孔雀羽毛浸在青蛙眼淚中10分鐘，
吹乾之後敷在雙眼上，保證能助你恢復視力！

Is this for real? How long will he has to cover his eyes for?

Two years.

......

真的嗎？
那他要敷多久？

2年。

What? Samba has to live blind for two years? How can this comic continue if that's the case?

Don't worry, there are still plenty of options...

Wah

甚麼？要森巴當兩年瞎子？
那這個漫畫如何繼續下去？

不用擔心，
還有很多方法……

哇~~~

First, the "Eye-clearing" massage!!

Argh~~~

Next, smoke therapy!!

首先，來個「明目」按摩！！　　　　呀～～　　　接着，煙燻治療！！

Finally, Samba must stay in a room full of green plants for three days and nights,

let his eyes get fully relaxed!

最後，森巴要留在滿佈
綠色植物的室內三日三夜，　　　　　　　　讓他的雙眼能
好好放鬆！

Grrrrr~~~

Grrrrr~~~

Ho Ho Ho Ho

Seems like torture...

Of course not, let me show you the result of this ancient therapy!

嘎～～　　　嘎～～　　　呵呵呵呵　　　看來是在虐待他……

當然不是，我來給你看看
原始療法的成果吧！

森巴，這個箭頭指向哪？

上

剛 我答得對不對？

哈哈，看來我的原始
療法沒有效……

對呀，你應該用現代方法，
去配一副眼鏡！

嗨！

你怎可以沒經同意就
走進別人的家裏？

是……是那個美女
開門讓我進來的……

我剛從雜貨店買東西回來，
這個阿伯就跟了我進屋，

他說自己是眼鏡推銷員，
想給我介紹他的新貨……

我視力正常，
不需要配眼鏡！

你何時做了
眼鏡推銷員？

要賺錢交租呀，只好甚麼
能賺取生計的事都做~

森巴你好，聽聞你近來視力不佳~

看，剛巧我有些
眼鏡可以給你試……

啊

剛巧？聽來
很可疑……

試試看吧，我的眼鏡全都有不同度數，
你會找到一副最適合你的眼鏡！

哦……

103

呵~~~

哈~~~

哈~~~

哇~~~

戴了那副眼鏡甚麼都看不見！
為甚麼拿它來賣？

那是用來隱藏外貌！讓你
不被人認出來，哈哈~~~

PA

啪一

None of your glasses suit Samba, I think it will be better if I take him out to buy one...

Ah

Wait a minute, I have a super special product!!

你的眼鏡沒有一副適合森巴，我還是帶他到外面買好了……

呀

等一等，我有一件超級特別產品!!

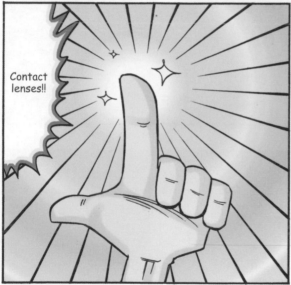

Contact lenses!!

隱形眼鏡!!

Ha~~~

Why don't I see anything?

I can't see a thing either...

哈~~~

為何我甚麼都沒看見？

我也甚麼都看不見……

That's right! This is a high-tech contact lens created with nanotechnology!!

Only truly smart people can see it!!

沒錯!!這個是用了納米技術造的高科技隱形眼鏡!!

只有真正聰明的人才看得到!!

Get out!!

滾開!!

別愚弄我們!!

砰—

我最討厭別人在屋裏
妨礙我做家務!!　阿伯,
你還好嗎?　放心,
他未死……　啊

Ha

Hey, don't stare at me like that...

You look weird with uncle's glasses on...

哈

喂，不要這樣盯着我……

你戴了阿伯的眼鏡後，樣子變得很怪……

Shoelace

is

loose

Huh? My shoelace is loose? But I'm wearing slipper with no shoelace at all...

掉鞋帶

吓？我掉鞋帶？但我穿拖鞋沒鞋帶呀……

Hm?

唔？

Oh!!

噢!!

What Samba saw was this fly!! Its shoelace is indeed loose...

原來森巴看到的是這蒼蠅!!牠的鞋帶確實掉了……

PA!!

How can Samba see in such amazing detail suddenly?

啪!!

為甚麼森巴忽然能看得那麼清楚？

屁股阿伯哈哈　　　　　　哇~~快還我眼鏡!!

呀~~~　　夠了!別再胡鬧!!
把眼鏡還給阿伯吧!

咦　　　　難道是阿伯的眼鏡讓森巴
的視力回復清晰?

我也試試看……

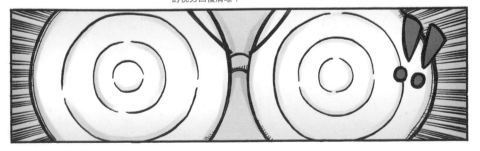

Wow!! Why does Samba look so handsome!?

Everything I see through these glasses look so different!!

哇!!為何森巴變帥了這麼多!?

戴上這副眼鏡後，東西看起來都變得很不一樣!!

Ha~~~ this is fascinating!

Kang, aren't you getting a little silly there?

My glasses~~~

哈~~~很有趣呀！

剛仔，你在那邊發傻嗎？

我的眼鏡呀~~~~

A story of dust
塵的故事

It is sunny today and the temperature is moderate.

Hi!!

It looks perfect for going out to play.

今天天氣晴朗，溫度適中。　　　　　　　　　　嗨!!　　　　　很適合出外遊玩。

Samba is preparing a big meal for lunch...

森巴正準備豐富的午餐……

The koalas who just ate are now starting their nine hour nap...

吃飽的樹熊也開始長達
九小時的午睡……

And Monkey is studying to enhance his knowledge...

馬騮不停看書
增進知識……

The teenage girl Cui Cui is continuing her frenzied shopping...

少女翠翠繼續瘋狂購物……

And Tiger-maru is still being chased by the rats...

虎丸繼續被老鼠追着跑……

All the animals are out for activities in the sun...

所有動物都在陽光下活動……

But only one man...

除了一個男人……

... stays quietly at home to protect the house where all find shelter...

……安靜地留在家裏，守護着眾人的棲身之所……

113

Yeah !!

Finally I am the protagonist of this chapter!!

耶!!　　　　　　　　　　　　　　　　　　　　　　　　　　　我終於成為本話的主角!!

It's been such a long time since I've been the protagonist. Don't you all miss me?

Let do my dance of celebration !!

Yo Yo~

Ha Ha~

我很久也沒有當主角。想我嗎?　　　　　　　　跳舞慶祝吧!!　　啲啲~~　　　哈哈~~

剛仔，你在那邊做甚麼？

全屋都很安靜，請你不要吵着我們玩紙牌遊戲。

給你2元⋯⋯出去玩吧!!

出去!!!

呼~ 終於安靜了⋯⋯

現在只有我一個在家，我要好好享受!!

首先，去廚房找食物!!

砰—

可惡!!他們出門前都不打掃,
要我一個人打掃!!

我真的不明白他們
怎樣弄髒的!!

咳咳⋯⋯　　　　咳咳咳⋯⋯

咳咳～～!!

呼~完成了!非常乾淨!!

為甚麼還有一大團灰塵!?

一定是我沒有掃乾淨， 掃走它吧!!

嗯？今天有那麼大風嗎？

好吧!! 呼呼— 用吸塵機!!

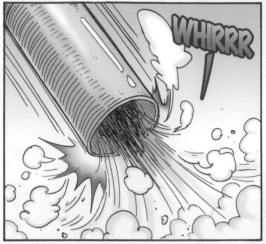

WHIRRR

呼呼—

Done!!

完成!!

PU

Ehhh ~~~!?

噗—　咦~~~!?

Why has the dust escaped!?

為何灰塵會逃走!?

Looks like the vacuum cleaner didn't work... Alright, let me use a more original method!!

可能是吸塵機壞了……好吧，
等我用最原始方法!!

Hey!!

嘿!!

可惡!!

不要動!!　　　　　啪一

我會抓到你，我發誓!!　　　嘎……嘎……

你惹我生氣了!!
試這方法!!

抓到了!! 啪— 嗖~

吼~ 我被一團灰塵耍弄了!!

啊~~ 嗖—

咦……

嘿嘿~ 終於抓到了……

用我的嘴接住…… 真的很噁心……

I have to spit this out as soon as possible and flush it away!!

我要儘快吐出來沖掉!!

PU!

Haaa...

噗— 乞……

Hachoooo~~!!

乞啾~~!!

What!? It ran out on its own!?

甚麼!?它跑掉了!?

T... This...

This is not a normal pile of dust~~~!!

這……這…… 這不是一團普通的灰塵~~~!!

121

難道是透明人的
惡作劇!?

又或者是森巴和馬騮
用遙控器控制!?

Ah!! I have an idea!

I can find information online!

啊!!我有辦法！

上網找資料！

Keyword... Dust-like animal...

關鍵字⋯⋯塵狀動物⋯⋯

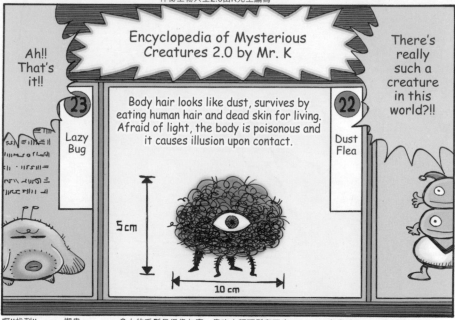

Encyclopedia of Mysterious Creatures 2.0 by Mr. K

神秘生物大全2.0由K先生編寫

Ah!! That's it!!

There's really such a creature in this world?!!

23 Lazy Bug

Body hair looks like dust, survives by eating human hair and dead skin for living. Afraid of light, the body is poisonous and it causes illusion upon contact.

5cm

10 cm

22 Dust Flea

啊!!找到!!

懶蟲

身上的毛髮長得像灰塵，靠吃人類頭髮和死皮生存。怕光，身體有毒，會令接觸者產生幻覺。

灰塵跳蚤

這個世界真的有這種生物嗎?!!

Cough~ Cough~ But it's poisonous!!

I even used my mouth to catch it... Bluhhh~~

咳~ 咳~ 但它有毒!!

我甚至用嘴接住它⋯⋯嘔~~

Hehe... But now I know what creature you are!!

I will definitely catch you this time! Round 2 begins!!

嘿嘿⋯⋯我知道你是甚麼生物了!!

這次我一定會抓到你！第二回合開始!!

Eh!? Where's that dust flea!? It was here just now!!

Why is there so much dust over there!?

Huh!?

咦!?灰塵跳蚤在哪裏!?
剛才還在這裏!!

為甚麼那邊有一團灰塵!?　啊!?

You are back!! And you helped me catch the dust!! You're so awesome!!

How have I helped you catch anything when I came back!?

Hi I am home

你們回來了!!還幫我
抓到灰塵!!你真棒!!

我剛回家，就要我
幫你抓住它!?

我回家了

This dust has been fooling around with me for a long time,

now you have nowhere to go anymore! Let me finish you!!

這團灰塵一直在耍弄我，

現在無處可逃了！
等我收拾你吧!!

Give it to me!!

給我!!

125

《大偵探福爾摩斯》DIY ①
跟着福爾摩斯做親子手作！

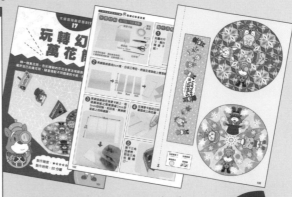

- 內含21個趣味親子DIY小手工。
- 有服裝、裝飾、交通工具、玩具、文具五大主題。
- 可作玩具和日常擺設。
- 每個都有詳細的步驟説明。

《大偵探福爾摩斯》
科學玩具① 螺旋槳雙翼機
親自裝嵌飛機，飛行方式由你定！

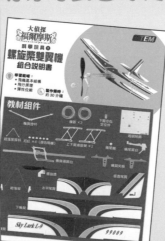

- 包含科學讀本乙冊及STEM玩具乙盒。
- 玩具雙翼機尺寸約 48 x 43 cm，附有清晰的組裝過程，跟着步驟就能完成裝嵌。
- 配合圖解，深入淺出說明飛行力學和飛行原理。
- 隨書還收錄了應用練習工作紙、科學漫畫，讓你一邊玩一邊接觸科學。

— MR. UNIVERSE! — ⑥

Artist : Keung Chi Kit

Concept : Rightman Creative Team

Chief Editor : Chan Ping Kwan

Editors : Kwok Tin Bo, So Wai Yee, Wong Suk Yee

Designers : Wong Cheuk Wing, Yip Shing Chi

First published in Hong Kong in 2021 by

Rightman Publishing Limited

2A, Cheung Lee Industrial Building, 9 Cheung Lee Street, Chai Wan, Hong Kong

Printed and bound by

Rainbow Printings Limited

3-4 Floor, 26-28 Tai Yau Street, San Po Kong, Kowloon, Hong Kong

Distributed by

Tung Tak Newspaper & Magazine Agency Co., Ltd.

Ground Floor, Yeung Yiu Chung No.5 Industrial Building, 34 Tai Yip Street,
Kwun Tong, Kowloon, Hong Kong
Tel: (852) 3551-3388   Fax: (852) 3551- 3300

ISBN:978-988-8504-32-9
HK$60 / NT$300

If damages or missing pages of the book are found, please
contact us by calling (852) 2515-8787.

On-line purchasing is easy and convenient.
Free delivery in Hong Kong for one purchase above HK$100.
For details, please visit www.rightman.net.